DOWN WITH THE ROMANS!

READZ⦿NE
ReadZone Books Limited

First published in this edition 2015

© copyright in the text Stewart Ross, 1997
© copyright in this edition ReadZone Books 2015

First published 1997 by Evans Brothers Ltd

The right of the Author to be identified as the Author of this work
has been asserted by the Author in accordance with the Copyright,
Designs and Patents Act 1988

Printed in Malta by Melita Press

Every attempt has been made by the Publisher to secure
appropriate permissions for material reproduced in this book.
If there has been any oversight we will be happy to rectify the
situation in future editions or reprints. Written submissions should
be made to the Publishers.

British Library Cataloguing in Publication Data (CIP) is available
for this title.

ISBN 978 1 78322 547 7

Visit our website: www.readzonebooks.com

DOWN
WITH THE ROMANS!

Stewart Ross

TO THE READER

Down with the Romans! is a story. It is based on history. The main events in the book really happened. But the details and some of the people are made up. I hope this makes the story more fun to read. I also hope that *Down with the Romans!* will get you interested in real history. When you have finished, perhaps you will want to find out more about Roman Britain!

Stewart Ross

THE STORY SO FAR ...

THE ROMANS

About 2000 years ago the Romans were the most powerful people in Europe. Their mighty armies defeated everyone who came against them. They gathered all their lands into an empire, ruled by the Roman emperor. The city of Rome, in Italy, was the capital of the empire.

Inside the Roman Empire there were fine roads and towns with magnificent buildings. The law protected Roman citizens, who enjoyed peaceful and comfortable lives. Much of the hard and dirty work was done by slaves.

For a long time Britain was not part of the Roman Empire.

THE BRITONS

Most of Britain was inhabited by tribes of people called Celts. Some of the best known tribes were the Iceni and the Trinovantes from East Anglia and the Catuvellauni, who lived in the Midlands. Each tribe had its own king or queen.

The Celts were farmers and warriors. They worshipped Nature and believed in magic. Their priests, called druids, were very powerful. The Celts had their own money and traded with the Romans. Instead of towns, they built huge forts on the tops of hills.

THE ROMAN CONQUEST

Julius Caesar was the first Roman general to come to Britain. He invaded twice, in 55 BC and 54 BC, but his armies did not stay long.

In 43 AD the Roman emperor Claudius decided to add Britain to his empire. Within a year, his large army had conquered most of southern England. Several tribes, such as the Iceni, made peace with the Romans. Towns and roads were built, and some Britons began to accept the Roman way of life.

By 60 AD, most of the Roman soldiers had moved north to conquer Wales. But all was not well in the areas they had left behind. In particular, Queen Boudicca of the Iceni was furious at the way the Romans were behaving …

BC (Before the birth of Jesus Christ)

About 450
The first Celts arrive in Britain

55
Julius Caesar's first visit to Britain

500	400	300	200	100

54
Julius Caesar's second visit to Britain

TIME LINE

AD (After the birth of Jesus Christ)

43
The Romans invade Britain

About 60
Boudicca's revolt

83 or 84
Romans win a great victory in Scotland but the Romans do not stay there

196
Barbarians attack over Hadrian's Wall

367–370
Many Barbarians attack Britain.
The Romans drive them off

0   100   200   300   400   500

About 400
Roman legions leave Britain.
Over the next 100 years tribes of
Angles, Saxons, Jutes and Scots
come to live in Britain

296
Barbarians attack again over Hadrian's Wall

About 122–130
Hadrian's Wall built across northern England

About 80
England is ruled as part of the Roman Empire

49
Romans set up a town at Colchester

PORTRAIT GALLERY

Boudicca
Queen of the Iceni

Mallia
Boudicca's eldest daughter

Druina
Boudicca's younger daughter

Gengix
the wise druid

Drimand
a Trinovantes warrior

Suetonius
the Roman governor

Catus
a Roman official

Cerialis
a Roman warrior

Chapter 1

BOUDICCA'S PROBLEM

The room was small and gloomy. Mallia and Druina sat huddled together beside an open fire in the middle of the earth floor. With sad, pale faces, they watched their mother pacing up and down like an animal in a cage.

After a while, Mallia broke the silence. 'What is it, mother?' she asked quietly. 'Please tell us!'

Queen Boudicca paused and looked down at her. 'I'm sorry, Mallia, but I just can't make up my mind what to do!'

'It's the Romans, isn't it?'

The queen nodded. 'Yes. Of course it's the Romans.'

She knelt down and took the girls in her arms. 'Oh my poor daughters! Nothing has gone right since your father died. You know how badly we have been treated. But it's not just us. It's the whole tribe. Everyone has had enough – the farmers and their wives, the druids and especially the traders.'

The thirteen-year-old Druina shivered and took her mother's hand. She wanted to forget what the Romans had done to her.

'You know, Druina', continued the queen kindly, 'Even the old fool who chases the crows off the cornfields is fed up. The other day, he decided to go to Rome to complain to the emperor. But he got so drunk at his farewell party that he didn't get past his own doorstep!'

Druina grinned and squeezed her mother's hand.

'And now', Boudicca said softly, 'Everyone is waiting for me to do something about it.' She sat down beside her daughters. 'There are times', she sighed, 'When I wish I wasn't queen of the Iceni.'

For a few minutes she stared into the fire, thinking of the happy years she had spent with her husband, King Prasutagus.

'It wasn't always like this', she remembered. 'When the first fighting was over, your father and I quite liked the Romans. We liked the careful way they organised things. We liked their wine and their jewellery. Your father's last piece of advice to me was to work with them. The future was bound to be Roman, he said.'

Boudicca paused. 'I wonder if he'd say that now?', she said quietly. 'Things have changed so much since your father died. The new Roman officials are nothing but greedy, heavy-handed bullies. They take our houses and land. They swagger about collecting taxes, beating people up and giving orders as if they own the place. Which they don't. Not all of it, anyway.'

Boudicca tapped her fingers together and frowned. 'I know what I want to do', she said. 'But is it right?'

Mallia was a thoughtful girl. When her mother had finished, she turned to her and said, 'You mustn't try to do everything on your own, mother. You need to talk to someone. You need advice.'

Boudicca stood up. 'You're right, Mallia. There's no point in hanging about. We must do something. Now!'

She went to the door and called for her maid.

The girl came quickly into the room. 'Yes, Your Majesty?'

'Listen, Accia, I am about to give you a very important task.'

Accia's eyes grew wider. 'Y-yes?', she stammered.

'This evening', whispered the queen, 'Just before dark, go into the woods, to the hut of Gengix the Wise. Tell him that Queen Boudicca wishes to speak with him at once.'

When Accia had gone, the queen returned to the fire.

'Thank you, Mallia', she said. 'We are beginning to get somewhere, at last. If the druid thinks as I do, we'll end the problem of the Romans – once and for all!'

Chapter 2

GENGIX'S ANSWER

Gengix the Wise was over eighty years old. He lived alone in a hut amid the oak trees of the forest. His eyes were bright and his beard was long and very white. He smelt of wood-smoke and herbs. More importantly, he was the cleverest man Boudicca had ever met.

'Yes, your majesty?' the old druid said, as he came into the room. 'You sent for me?'

'I did', replied Boudicca. She was a proud woman and did not like what she had to say next. But she knew it had to be done. She took a deep breath. 'I need help.'

The druid fixed his sharp blue eyes on her. 'I know.'

Boudicca was startled. 'You know?'

Gengix smiled. 'That is why you sent for me, presumably.' He sat down cross-legged on the floor. 'Tell me all about it, O Queen of the great Iceni.'

So Boudicca told him.

She told him how her husband Prasutagus left half his kingdom to the Roman emperor and half to his daughters, Mallia and Druina. But the new governor, Suetonius, had taken all of it. And Catus, the official in charge of their part of the country, wanted all their money as well.

Roman soldiers had treated Mallia and Druina terribly. And she – a queen! – had been beaten. She showed Gengix the scars on her shoulder. In the past the Iceni had worked with the Romans in the hope of a better life. Now it looked as if they would have no life at all. They had lost everything. Many of them were slaves.

Boudicca stood up and began pacing the room again.

'My people have reached breaking point, Gengix!' she cried. 'Every day they come and beg me to do something. I have tried talking with the Romans, but they don't listen. Last time, they laughed in my face. One of the guards even spat at me and called me barbarian!'

The queen spun round. 'Well, Gengix', she demanded, 'What shall I do?'

The druid took a deep breath. 'What would your husband have done, Boudicca?'

'Prasutagus? He would not have put up with ...'

She did not finish. At that moment, the door burst open and four burly Roman soldiers marched in. They were armed to the teeth.

'I beg your pardon ...' the queen began.

The officer in charge pushed her out of the way. 'Shut up, barbarian!' he shouted. He pointed at Gengix. 'That's the one! Seize him!'

Two soldiers grabbed Gengix by his arms. The third pulled him to his feet by the hair.

'Right, you wrinkled old fool!' barked the officer. 'You're under arrest. Suspicious behaviour. And if you try to resist, I'll break every bone in your scrawny body!'

He turned to Boudicca. 'And if you make so much as one squeak of complaint, barbarian, it'll be your daughters. Again!'

Gengix said nothing. But as he was being dragged away, he gave Boudicca one final, fiery glance. The look said everything. The queen had the answer she wanted.

That night Boudicca sent out messengers. They galloped through the dark, along paths not known to the Romans. They went to the chiefs of her own people, the Iceni, and to the Trinovantes and other tribes in the east of England.

Their message was clear. The Romans were no longer welcome in England. They had betrayed the people's trust and must be driven out by force. If the leaders of the other tribes agreed, Boudicca would lead them in revolt against the Romans. But for the moment, there must be the utmost secrecy.

The queen was tired but excited when she finally went to bed that night. For a while she lay awake, thinking. She had done her duty. There could be no turning back. But had she made the right decision? Was war really the answer?

Only time would tell ....

Chapter 3

IN THE VALLEY OF THE COLNE

Boudicca's call to war was just what the tribes had been waiting for. They accepted her as leader and arranged to meet on the night of the full moon in the Colne Valley, above the Roman town of Colchester.

Over the next few days, Boudicca was busier than she had ever been in her life. With her daughters at her side, she travelled around in a chariot calling her people to arms. Cheering crowds greeted her wherever she went. Each day her army grew stronger. There was not a Roman to be seen. As soon as they heard what was going on, they fled to the south.

The whole countryside was alive with preparations. The druids prayed and made sacrifices to the gods, asking for their help. Male and female warriors took out their rusty old swords for polishing and sharpening. They fitted new shafts to their spears and new wheels to their chariots. On the morning Boudicca left for Colchester, she commanded 50,000 ferocious, fully-armed soldiers.

The full moon was rising above the trees when they reached the River Colne. Hundreds of camp-fires dotted the tree-lined slopes. By their yellow light, Boudicca made out the dark shapes of her army – men, women, horses, chariots and even a few children gathered beside the leaping flames.

Boudicca pitched camp and summoned the leaders to join her in a council of war. When they arrived, she climbed into her chariot and addressed them.

'Fellow warriors', she began, looking round at them in the moonlight, 'Tomorrow, at first light, we march on Colchester. We shall not stop until the last Roman is driven from our land. But, friends, I beg you to be merciful as well as brave. Cruelty is the Roman way, not ours.

'Now return to your people and prepare for battle. Soldiers of Britain, if the gods are with us, we shall conquer! In the name of freedom and justice, we shall win!'

The chiefs gave Boudicca a great cheer then drifted off into the night. As she watched them go, Boudicca was worried. They were a rough and bloodthirsty lot who would certainly fight like lions. But she was not sure they would heed her call for mercy.

'Mother!' Mallia's voice called in the darkness. 'Mother, there's someone here to see you.'

Boudicca woke up. It was still dark and her blanket was wet with dew. She reached for her sword. 'Who is it?' she whispered.

'Do not fear, O Queen', a young voice replied. 'My name does not matter. It is my message you must hear.'

Boudicca rubbed her eyes. Beside the fire she saw the dim outline of a woman. She was wrapped in a heavy shawl and her face was in shadow.

'A message?', the queen asked. 'Who from? Is it important?'

'Listen, mighty Boudicca', the woman hissed. 'Turn back now, before it is too late. You are leading your people to death and terrible destruction.'

Boudicca tried to interrupt. The speaker lifted her hand and continued.

'Though the Romans have done you wrong, Boudicca, you cannot defeat them. Even if you kill all the Romans in Britain, more will come from over the seas. Then more and more. Other brave warriors have tried to stop them. They have failed, as you too will fail. Save your people, O Queen! Turn back! Turn back!'

With these words, the figure disappeared into the darkness. Boudicca sent men to find her, but they returned empty handed.

Just some old fool, the queen told herself as she lay down again to sleep. Of course we can win! But the woman's words haunted her for the rest of the night. She was glad when dawn came and she could busy herself for the battle ahead.

Chapter 4

COLCHESTER

The British set out at dawn. Although Boudicca did her best to get the warriors properly organized, they were too excited to take much notice. But they did agree not to attack Colchester until everyone was ready.

The army was in good spirits as it threaded its way through the trees. Some of the men were boasting about what they would do to the Romans. It was not pretty talk. To her left Boudicca heard a band of farmers singing.

'Death to the Romans! Chuck 'em in the ditch!

We'll take their money, and we'll be rich!'

The queen was alarmed. They seemed to be looking forward to plundering Colchester more than driving out the Romans.

The first Britons reached Colchester a couple of hours after sunrise. Behind its low earth walls, the town was very still. As the rest of the army arrived, it spread out through the fields on either side of the river. It was a beautiful summer's day and the sun glinted brightly on their polished weapons.

When all was ready, Boudicca climbed into her chariot and raised her sword. After muttering a quick prayer to the gods, she lowered her sword and shouted in a loud voice:

'Down – with – the – Ro – mans!'

The battle cry was taken up the whole army: 'Down with the Romans! Down with the Romans!'

Then, like a stampede of wild animals, the Britons charged.

The people of Colchester – Roman and British – did not stand a chance. Within five minutes, Boudicca's soldiers were over the walls and running through the streets, yelling and swearing like madmen. They burst into the houses, killing everyone they found – even the children. They broke into shops and stole money and goods. They smashed the statues, set fire to the government offices and held a huge party in the theatre.

Smoke and screams filled the air.

There were only a few Roman soldiers in Colchester. Realizing they could not defend the walls, they barricaded themselves in the temple. For two days they held out. But in the end the British broke through and set the building alight. The last few Romans died in the flames.

Boudicca's army gathered to watch the blaze. The temple was dedicated to worship of the emperor. It stood for everything they hated about the conquerors. When the roof finally caved in, the Britons let out a great cheer of delight.

Once the battle was over, Boudicca did not know whether to laugh or cry.

'Aren't you happy, mother?' Mallia asked when they

were alone together. 'After all, you have won a great victory.'

Boudicca put an arm round the girl's shoulders. 'Yes, I am happy, Mallia. We have set our people free. But I am sad, too.'

'Why?'

'All that violence and cruelty. Don't you see, we are behaving just like the enemy! Besides, one victory does not win the war. The Romans will be back, you can be sure of that.'

'But mother!' Mallia cried. 'We can't stop now!'

'Of course', Boudicca agreed. 'The revolt must go on.'

But she was haunted by the words of the woman beside the camp-fire. Whoever she was, she was right.

A fight with the Romans meant a fight to the death.

Chapter 5

THE SOLDIERS OF ROME

Once the slaughter had finished and the soldiers had recovered from their wild rejoicing, Boudicca called the army leaders together. They met in the ruins of the theatre to decide what to do next.

The queen argued that they would not be safe until they had defeated the main Roman armies. 'We must go north to find them', she explained. 'And when we find them, we will defeat them in battle. Then, and only then, we shall be truly free.'

Most of the Iceni chiefs agreed with her. But Drimand, a huge warrior of the Trinovantes tribe, put forward a different plan.

'Our families are poor', he growled, rising to his feet. 'They want back what the Romans have stolen. They will not find it in the purses of the Roman legionaries, but in the towns. We must attack the towns and grow rich!'

The Trinovantes sitting near him muttered in agreement.

Boudicca walked over to him and smiled. 'I understand your worry, Drimand', she said quietly. 'But one day we will have to fight the legions. The sooner the better, I say, before they get help from Rome.'

Drimand shook his head. 'No, Boudicca. Help will

not come yet. We must take towns. When the news of what we are doing spreads, other Britons will join us. Soon our army will be so strong that all the legions in the empire will not be able to beat us!'

It was a good speech, and even some of the Iceni seemed to agree with it. Boudicca felt she was losing the argument.

At that moment, they heard shouts coming down outside the theatre. Seconds later a young man stumbled into the meeting. His clothes were torn. His face was bathed in sweat.

'Boudicca!' he panted. 'Queen Boudicca, I have urgent news!'

The meeting went quiet. Everyone leaned forward to hear what he had to say.

'The Romans! The Romans are coming! An army under the command of Cerialis is on its way here. Now!'

Drimand held up his hand. 'Are you sure?'

'I saw them with my own eyes, sir. I only just escaped with my life.'

Drimand turned to Boudicca. 'Well, Commander', he said with a smile, 'It looks as if you will have your way after all! First, we must fight the legions. Then we can move on to the towns!'

Boudicca shook him warmly by the hand. 'So be it, Drimand. And with you on our side, I pity those poor Romans!'

Cerialis was confident. As soon as he heard of Boudicca's attack on Colchester, he left his base in the

Midlands and marched to meet the rebels. He had only half the Ninth Legion at his command. But that was quite enough, he told his men. Who was frightened by a few barbarians led by a woman? The Romans were the best soldiers in the world. They would make mincemeat of anyone who got in their way.

Meanwhile, Boudicca's spies told her exactly where the Romans were and in what direction they were heading. She led her army out of Colchester towards the East Anglian Heights. There, in the wooded hills, the Britons prepared their ambush.

The Romans reached the spot in the late afternoon. They were tired after their long march and looking forward to setting up camp. Suddenly, the trees on either side of them burst into life. Thousands of warriors, some on foot and some in war chariots, sprang out of hiding and charged forward uttering bloodthirsty cries.

Cerialis ordered the alarm to be sounded. The cavalry wheeled about in disorder. The foot-soldiers tried to form up in defensive formation. But before they could do so, the enemy was upon them.

The battle raged until nightfall. Swords clashed, men screamed, horses whinnied. The legionaries fought bravely but they were heavily outnumbered. Dashing chariots cut great gaps in their ranks. Spears and clubs rained down upon them.

In the end, seeing that all was lost, Cerialis sounded the retreat. He fled to the north, surrounded by the remains of his cavalry. The legionaries were left to their fate.

Every single one of them was killed.

Later that evening, Boudicca left her warriors to their celebrations and walked out onto the battlefield. To her surprise, she saw a man standing alone among the bodies strewn on the ground. It was Drimand.

For a while they stood together looking at the bloody scene. Eventually Drimand spoke. 'This was a great victory, Boudicca. You must be very proud.'

'I am', replied the queen. 'But I am also sad that all these brave men had to die. Thank you for your help, Drimand.'

The warrior shrugged. 'Don't thank me! We had to win, didn't we? Otherwise you would not lead us on to London.'

'London?' Boudicca asked. 'Is that where you want to go?'

'Yes. On to London. Then Verulamium. Then who knows where? Perhaps even Rome itself! Do you fancy yourself as an empress, Boudicca?'

'No, Drimand. Not an empress. I just want to be queen of the Iceni. Living in peace once more.'

Chapter 6

LONDON AND VERULAMIUM

London and Verulamium suffered the same fate as Colchester. Boudicca's followers stole everything they could lay their hands on and took no prisoners. When citizens surrendered, the Britons executed them most cruelly. Houses, offices, shops and temples were burned to the ground.

Afterwards, the British were so weighed down with loot that they looked more like pedlars than soldiers. They had rows of rings on their fingers. Bangles, necklaces and brooches clinked and jingled as they walked. Many had bags of coin slung over their shoulders or hanging from their waists. Some of them had taken so much that they needed wagons to carry it all.

Hearing what was going on, thousands more warriors joined the rebels. Boudicca now had more than 100,000 soldiers at her command. Many women came along too, eager to be with their husbands. They brought their children with them and rode behind their men in the wagons.

The army had turned into a huge caravan of gypsy warriors.

Boudicca was uneasy. She was sick of all the burning and killing. She wanted to get the revolt over as quickly as possible so that everyone could return home. After the destruction of London, she had a long talk with Drimand.

'It's time we marched against the legions of Governor Suetonius', she argued. 'As you know, he's on his way south from Wales with a large force.'

Drimand was not at all helpful. 'My warriors will fight the Romans when they show up', he snorted. 'In the meantime, we need more loot.'

So Boudicca had to wait. And with every day that passed, the legions moved closer.

By the time the British finally left the smoking ruins of Verulamium behind them and set out to find Suetonius, the summer was drawing to a close. The nights were longer and colder. Dark rain clouds hung in the sky for days on end. The wagons got stuck in the muddy tracks and even the chariot drivers found the going tough. Slowly, very slowly, Boudicca's gigantic army advanced towards the enemy.

One evening, a messenger came running into Boudicca's camp.

'Your Majesty', he gasped, 'I bring good news. Gengix the druid is alive and well! One of our bands found him in a fort and set him free. He's coming to join you as quickly as he can.'

Boudicca was delighted and straight away went to tell Drimand. 'We need his advice', she said. 'Let's hope he gets here before we meet the legions.'

'Oh Boudicca!' he cried. 'You are such a worrier! Everything's going to be all right. I promise!'

Chapter 7

THE GOLDEN RULE OF WAR

Gengix reached Boudicca's camp two days later. He seemed older and thinner than before, but he was in good health and keen to help.

'Tell me what you know of the enemy, O Queen', he asked. 'Where are they now and what are their numbers?' They were sitting on rugs in Boudicca's tent. Rain dripped from a small hole in the roof.

The queen told him all she knew. Suetonius, the Roman governor of Britain, had left London just before the rebels arrived. He had gone north to collect more troops and was now returning with about 10,000 legionaries. British spies reported they were about a day's march away.

'Your army is much bigger than his', the druid noted. He stared hard at Boudicca as he spoke.

'I know', she replied. 'But ...' She was remembering how well Cerialis' small force had fought.

Gengix read her thoughts. 'Yes. The Romans are fine soldiers. It will not be an easy victory.'

'We shall win?' Boudicca asked.

'Only the gods know the future, O Queen. But listen to the last advice of Gengix the Wise. This is the golden rule of war: Never do what your enemy wants.'

Boudicca was puzzled. 'What do you mean?'

'If Suetonius prepares his legions for battle, you must not fight. He will be ready for you. Fight when you want to and where you want to. That way you will win.'

'That is how we defeated Cerialis', said Boudicca.

'Yes', Gengix replied. 'And that is how you will defeat Suetonius.'

Drimand came to see Boudicca early the next morning. He was in an excellent mood.

'We've got them now!', he called as he burst into the queen's tent. 'Rats in a trap, Boudicca! Rats in a trap!'

'What on earth do you mean, Drimand? And where have you been? You look dreadful!'

The Trinovantine grabbed a loaf of bread and began wolfing it down. Between bites, he explained that he had been out spying all night. He had seen the Romans with his own eyes. They were at one end of a long valley, with woods at their rear, waiting for the British to attack.

'So you see', he finished, 'They are trapped. Today we move up to the other end of the valley. Tomorrow we charge and wipe them off the face of the earth!'

He took a swig of wine from a stone jug. 'The gods are on our side, Boudicca. Victory will be ours! We shall set our people free!'

For a moment, the queen made no reply. Then she said slowly, 'The golden rule of war is: Never do what your enemy wants.'

Drimand laughed. 'We all know that! Do you think Suetonius' paltry force wants to fight? We have twenty times more soldiers than them. Suetonius knows he hasn't got a chance. That's why he has the woods behind him – so he can run away and hide when he has lost!'

Drimand spoke for all the warriors. They wanted a battle and they were sure of victory. Boudicca knew she could not stop them.

'Drimand, are you certain we can win?' she asked.

'Absolutely certain!'

'Very well', she replied slowly. 'Tell the army to advance. Tomorrow we will fight the greatest battle of our lives.'

All day the mighty British army struggled through the damp countryside towards the battlefield that Suetonius had chosen. Gengix rode beside Boudicca in her chariot. He did not say much. But when they reached the end of the valley and saw the smoke of the Roman camp fires in the distance, he took out a small bottle from inside his tunic.

'Here, O Queen', he said, handing the bottle to her. 'Take this, just in case. I pray to the gods that you will not need it.'

Boudicca's eyes filled with tears as she thanked him. The druid did not tell her what was in the bottle. She knew.

The queen did not sleep well that night. She dreamed of the young woman who had come to her camp before Colchester. 'Turn back!' she warned once more. 'Turn back!'

Boudicca recognized the voice at once. To her horror, she realised it was her own.

Chapter 8

THE LAST BATTLE

The Britons were ready for battle shortly after dawn.

Boudicca divided her followers into three groups. At the front were the brightly painted war chariots. A vast array of warriors stood behind them, ready to charge. There were so many it was impossible to count. Druina tried and reckoned there were more than 150,000 soldiers.

They carried a terrifying collection of weapons – swords, spears, clubs, bows and arrows, slings and knives. Many men had painted their bodies with blue warpaint. As Boudicca rode among them, encouraging them to fight bravely, her heart beat faster. Not even the Romans, she thought, could defeat such a mighty force.

The wagons were arranged like grandstands behind the warriors. Women and children clambered over them, trying to find good positions to watch the battle.

Once more Boudicca drove her chariot to the head of her forces. She raised her sword. The army fell silent, waiting for the signal. 'Down – with – the – Ro – mans!' she screamed.

Down came the sword. Like a gigantic wave of steel, the Britons charged up the slope towards the enemy.

Boudicca watched the attack from a low mound on

one side of the valley. Her daughters stood beside her. Druina jumped up and down with excitement. Mallia stood very still staring at the battle with wide blue eyes.

The chariots thundered down the valley at great speed. Then, fifty paces before the Roman line, they stopped. Several toppled over.

'Mother!' screamed Druina. 'The chariots have fallen into a ditch!'

She was right. Knowing he was going to be attacked by chariots, Suetonius had got his men to dig a ditch across the valley. The chariot attack was useless.

Shortly afterwards, the British foot-soldiers reached the ditch. Some began lifting the chariots across, others ran on towards the Romans. When they still had twenty yards to go, a trumpet blared. A black cloud of javelins rose into the air and fell among the Britons. The charge halted. Men ran about in all directions, trying to escape the hail of deadly missiles.

A second trumpet sounded. The legionaries moved into a wedge formation and marched forward. For over an hour the two armies met in fierce hand-to-hand fighting. All the time the Romans kept up their advance, stabbing viciously from behind their broad shields.

Druina turned her head away. Tears rolled down her cheeks.

When the legionaries reached the ditch, she heard a third trumpet call.

Mallia pointed down the valley. 'Oh no!' she gasped. 'Look! Cavalry!'

From either side of the Roman line, horsemen swooped into the valley, attacking the Britons from behind. The slaughter was terrible. Soon the remains of Boudicca's army was fleeing towards the wagons.

The cavalry set off in pursuit. Trapped between the wagons and the enemy, the Britons were cut to pieces. The legionaries came up and joined in the massacre. No one was spared. Warriors, women and children were all put to the sword.

In the chaos, Boudicca caught a glimpse of Drimand. He was standing on a wagon, desperately swinging his great sword. Shortly afterwards, the Romans closed in and he fell to the ground.

Boudicca could watch no more. 'Come, daughters', she said. 'Follow me!'

She turned quickly and ran up the slope towards the trees.

The wood was damp and strangely peaceful. The noise of the battle sounded far away. Druina was crying quietly.

Boudicca took out the small bottle Gengix had given her. 'Here', she said, 'Take a sip of this. It will make you feel better.'

Druina wiped her eyes. 'What is it?'

Boudicca handed her the bottle. 'Just medicine. Gengix gave it to me.'

The girl put the bottle to her lips and drank.

'Ugh! It's horrible!' she whispered. Seconds later, she sank to the ground.

Boudicca gave the bottle to Mallia. 'You too, my love. Come, drink!'

Mallia hesitated.

'Do you want to be captured by the Romans?' Boudicca asked softly. The girl shook her head and drank.

When Mallia fell beside her sister, the queen wept. 'O my children!' she sobbed. 'O my people! What have I done?'

With these words, she drained the bottle of poison and lay down on the wet autumn leaves to die beside her daughters.

THE HISTORY FILE

WHAT HAPPENED NEXT?

Suetonius showed no mercy after Boudicca's death. Helped by fresh troops from Germany, he destroyed the farms and houses of every tribe that had sent warriors to her army. All over southern and eastern England, he burned villages and killed the inhabitants.

The governor's terrible revenge did not end the revolt. Without food or shelter, the Britons had nothing to lose. They fought on. Many hid in the woods and dashed out to attack the Romans whenever they could.

News of Suetonius' behaviour reached Rome. The emperor Nero sent top officials to see what was going on. They reported back to the capital and shortly afterwards Suetonius was replaced. The new governor was a wise and kindly man. The legions stopped their cruelty and the British tribes settled down. For the next three hundred years the whole of southern Britain lived in peace.

The Romans never conquered all Britain. They advanced into Scotland several times, winning great victories and building roads and forts. But they did not stay. Two huge walls marked the frontier of the Roman Empire and kept out the barbarians to the north.

The emperor Hadrian ordered the largest of these walls to be built. Hadrian's Wall ran for 80 miles across northern England. It was built of stone, with a large ditch on the northern side and forts every mile.

South of Hadrian's Wall the people flourished under Roman rule. Many towns and roads were built and the country grew rich. From the east came a new religion, Christianity. Many citizens thought Britain was one of the most pleasant places in the whole empire.

But the Roman empire could not last for ever. By 400 AD barbarian tribes were attacking it on every side. The legions left Britain to defend other regions. Not long afterwards, the Roman way of life had disappeared.

HOW DO WE KNOW?

It is very difficult to find out exactly what happened during Boudicca's revolt. We do not know, for example, where she fought her final battle. We do not even know what she looked like. Two Roman writers described the revolt, but they did not give much detail. They were both quite biased.

Tacitus (born in about 55 AD) wrote two accounts of the revolt. But since he was only four or five when it happened, we cannot be sure that he got things right. The other writer, Cassius Dio, was born a century after Boudicca's death. His history is even more inaccurate.

Historians try to fill the gaps in their knowledge with archaeology. For example, at the hill fort in South Cadbury, Somerset, archaeologists found the remains of bodies and weapons. They think the fort might have been destroyed by Suetonius. If they are right, then the governor took his revenge on tribes far from where the revolt had started.

Tacitus' accounts of Boudicca's revolt are not the same as Dio's. For example, Tacitus says that the final battle did not last long. Dio says the Romans took some time to defeat the Britons. Historians have to make up their own minds which to believe. They have to interpret the different accounts.

The Roman writers disagree on other matters. They both say Boudicca escaped after the battle. Tacitus believed she took poison. Dio says she died of illness. Which writer does this story follow?

NEW WORDS

AD
After the birth of Jesus Christ.

BC
Before the birth of Jesus Christ.

Barbarian
The Roman word for someone living outside their empire.

Cavalry
Soldiers on horseback.

Celts
The people living in most of Britain when the Romans came.

Council
A meeting.

Druid
A Celtic priest.

East Anglia
The eastern part of England.

Emperor
A man who rules an empire.

Empire
A large area ruled by one country.

Empress
A woman who rules an empire.

Governor
A person in charge of part of a country or empire.

Iceni
Boudicca's tribe.

Invade
Attack a country.

Legion
A large group of Roman soldiers, between 3000 and 5000 men.

Legionary
A Roman foot-soldier.

Pedlar
A person who travels from place to place selling things.

Plunder
Take goods by force.

Sling
A weapon for throwing stones.

Tax
Money given to the government.

Slaughter
Killing.

Temple
A building for worship.

Trinovantes
The tribe that join the Iceni in revolt against the Romans.

Tyranny
Cruel and unfair government.